sleepover

Adapted by Suzanne Weyn
Based on the story and screenplay by Elisa Bell

SO-AUZ-291

SCHOLASTIC INC.

New York   Toronto   London   Auckland   Sydney

Mexico City   New Delhi   Hong Kong   Buenos Aires

ISBN 0-439-65787-3

12 11 10 9 8 7 6 5 4 3 2   4 5 6 7 8 9/0

Printed in the U.S.A.
First printing, June 2004

Julie

I looked around the halls of Fielding Junior High. Notebook paper sailed through the air as kids emptied their lockers. One by one, boom boxes turned on. It was the last day of school before summer vacation. And, for me, it was also my final half hour in eighth grade — the end of my entire junior high career.

As I walked down the hall toward my locker, I can't say I was broken-hearted to be leaving. The junior high experience hadn't exactly been an overwhelming success for me. I wasn't wildly popular, my crush didn't even know I was alive, and my only moment of fame had been as the ugly step-sister in the spring production of *Cinderella*.

I opened my locker door, revealing the dreamy, romantic pictures taped inside. My whole door was covered with pictures of guys and girls, all of them lip-locked and in love. You might say that I was obsessed with kissing.

Unfortunately, not *one* of the girls in any of the pictures was me. My best friend, Hannah Jenkins, joined me at my locker. I stared at my romantic pictures one more second before turning toward her. "I'm destined never to be kissed," I said with a tragic sign.

"Don't be so dramatic," Hannah replied in a matter-of-fact tone. It was easy for *her* to say! Hannah is beautiful and confident. She sparkles. Boys were just dying to kiss *her*.

My English teacher, Mr. Corrado, hurried down the hall, handing out fat packets of paper to all the eighth-graders. "What's this?" I asked him when he handed a pack to Hannah and one to me. "I thought we were done with junior high."

"It's the summer reading list," he told us.

It was really long — nearly twenty pages! "Have *you* read all these books?" I asked him.

"Many times," he replied with a smile.

"Really, Mr. Corrado," Hannah said, "you need to get out more."

Mr. Corrado just laughed good-naturedly. He didn't seem offended. Truthfully, he was one of the best and nicest teachers I'd had at Fielding, even if he did exhibit-certain nerdy tendencies. He spotted some other eighth graders and hurried off to give them their reading lists.

My friend Farrah rushed up to Hannah and me at my locker. "Party problem," she reported grimly. I knew she was talking about my end-of-school slumber party.

Farrah reached into the pocket of her fringed, hippie-style skirt and pulled out a party invitation designed to look like an orange Popsicle. On the front it said: LIZ'S SLUMBER BLOWOUT. "Dueling parties," she said.

This *did* present a problem. I'd made a bold move and

invited Staci to my party. Long ago, back in grade school, we'd been friends. But in junior high she'd risen to the top of the social ladder while I sort of floated around somewhere in the middle — the lower middle. It wasn't as though I was a major geek or anything, just not super popular like blond, beautiful Staci.

"You can count Staci out of your party," Hannah said, which I'd already figured out. "She'll go to Liz's spread, for sure. It'll be much better for her image, and you know she's the image queen."

I checked over my shoulder and saw Staci and Liz at their lockers across the hall from mine. While Liz pulled out nail polish and fuzzy pink sweaters from her locker, Staci stared into her locker mirror and coated her lips with raspberry lip gloss. She had a picture of her hottie high school football star boyfriend taped to the gloss container.

"I wish I was her," someone said wistfully from one locker away. We turned and looked at a girl named Yancy. When Yancy realized we were staring at her, she blushed red. "Did I say that out loud?" she asked.

"Your mind leaked," I teased in a whisper.

I didn't really know her that well, but I'd seen her around school and she seemed nice. "We won't tell," I added with a smile. After all, she'd only expressed the way we *all* secretly felt.

Liz finished clearing out her locker and turned toward us. "Hey, Yancy," she called. "My father's a lawyer."

Yancy smiled nervously, not quite believing that the mega-popular Liz had actually spoken to her. "Oh?" she asked.

Liz shot her a nasty smile. "He could help you sue that diet company for non-performance."

I glanced at Yancy's backpack and noticed a pack of diet pills. I thought that what Liz had said was pretty mean, but Liz and Staci thought it was hysterical. They laughed and high-fived one another. Yancy was a little heavy, but just a little.

She looked completely devastated. I felt so sorry for her. Luckily there was still a small stack of computer-made party invitations in my locker. Impulsively, I pulled one out and held it out to her. "Yancy, want to come to my sleep-over?" I asked. My mom had said I could only invite three friends, but it was pretty certain that Staci wouldn't be coming, and I just *had* to do something to make this moment better for Yancy.

Yancy's crushed looked turned into a smile. "Me? Sure?" she replied. "Yes! Absolutely."

I smiled back at her, and, for that moment, I felt like I'd fixed the whole world. "It's tonight, sixish," I told her.

That warm, fuzzy feeling ended abruptly when Russell Alterman crashed into my locker, sending his hand-painted skateboard sailing up into the air.

Russell is definitely a mondo-dweeb, but *he* couldn't care less. He thinks he looks awesome in his big shorts, overdone wristband, and blue braces. He lives in Russell-land where he's king of his world. "Last chance to see a picture of me in a coma," he announced. "I've got tubes in nasty places."

That was an opportunity I could definitely pass up. "You were *barely* in a coma," I reminded him.

"Three hours," he insisted proudly, as if it had been a great accomplishment.

"You're such a mega-lame," Hannah told him. "Who runs into a bus with their skateboard?"

"A *parked* bus," Farrah added.

Russell shrugged, not at all embarrassed by their comments. "I missed the turn," he said.

"Clearly," I remarked. Two of Russell's geeky friends, Lance and Miles, boarded up to us. These two mini-uncools had the same annoying, "I'm-great" attitude as Russell. If they didn't have different skateboards a person might not be able to tell them apart. They high-fived, then low-fived, spun around, and did it all over again.

When all the hand slapping ended, Russell spied the invitations in my locker and snatched up one of them. "Hey, hey, what's this?" he said as he read it over. "Having a par-*tay* tonight?"

"Par-tay at Julie's!" Lance shouted.

"Don't even," I told Russell as I tried to grab the invitation back from him. He yanked it away from me, holding it in the air. Laughing, he boarded away with his pals, clutching the invitation in his hands.

Hannah

Julie and I walked out of school, heading toward home. On the way, we passed Abbott High School, just as we always did. The high school kids were just getting out. It was also their last day of school. We peered through the front gate into the courtyard that was the school's outside lunch area. "So this is our future," Julie said.

"Your future," I reminded her.

Julie looked slightly ill as she turned to me. "I can't believe you're moving," she said. "How am I supposed to do high school without you?

We were such close friends. I couldn't imagine life without her, either. I didn't know what to say, so I didn't say anything.

A girl laughed loudly from inside the gate of Abbott High. We turned, distracted by her laughter. She was standing by a fountain at the center where the obviously popular kids — with their letter sweaters and cheerleader outfits — hung out. "There it is, the lunch spot," I said.

"And there's where *I'll* be eating," Julie said, pointing to the tables next to the dumpsters. Kids who were clearly *not* cool sat there.

"Well . . . everybody knows Staci and Liz pretty much have a lock on the fountain," I admitted.

"Life is so predictable, it kills me," Julie muttered. She believed that the cool kids would always be cool and she would always be . . . well . . . not. And, as if to prove it was true, just then we noticed Staci leaning against a nearby tree kissing her quarterback boyfriend, Todd. "Case in point," Julie went on as she looked at Staci.

I wished Julie would lighten up. In elementary school she hadn't been so down on herself. But the social pressures at Fielding Junior High had really chipped away at her self-esteem. She's cute, smart and fun. The sad thing was that she didn't know it at all.

My attention was drawn away from Staci and her kissing show. I'd caught sight of a high school guy who stood on his skateboard on the wall around the school.

Julie was staring up at him too. "Steve is so plush," she murmured, which didn't surprise me. I knew she had a major crush on Steve Phillips. She'd gotten stuck on him back when he was also in junior high.

"He's okay if you like that sort of thing," I replied. The grunge-handsome, skater-boy-type isn't really my kind of guy. He was totally Julie's type, though.

Steve began speeding along the top of the wall. In the next second, he'd launched himself into the air and was sailing over and across the fountain. He landed smoothly on the opposite wall.

All the kids on the ground applauded, including Julie. She looked up at him with dreamy eyes.

He got down from the wall and skated out the front gate, right past us. "Isn't it great," Julie said, sounding bitter. "He can't see me, not at all."

I hated when she talked like this, all hopeless and sarcastic. "End the cliché!" I told her. "Just go up and talk to him." He had stopped at the curb to speak to some of his pals. This was her chance.

Julie just shook her head. "You're mistaking me for someone else — someone with courage and a short hem."

I shot her a look. I *so* wished she could see how attractive she really was!

As we headed for the Jamba Juice hangout next to the high school, Staci went by in the passenger seat of Todd's convertible. The car suddenly stopped, and Todd backed up to us. "Jules," Staci spoke to Julie. "I can't make your overnighter. I'm doing the dance."

"The dance?" Julie asked, not understanding what Staci meant.

Staci tilted her head and gave Julie a look that said *duh*. "The high school dance," she explained.

"Oh, right. Of course, have fun," Julie replied. Staci blew an orange bubble from her gum and let it pop as Todd sped off. "Have fun!" Julie repeated in a high, wimpy voice, mocking herself.

Julie and I started walking home once again. "So, I think

I have a solution," she said after a few minutes. "I'll just move with you."

I assumed she was joking, but she sure sounded serious. "My mom will have to find someone new to haunt. My dad will never actually notice I'm gone," she went on. "And Ren will — who really cares what my repeater brother does?" Ren was Julie's older brother, who had recently dropped out of college and returned home.

"You have to stay put, kiddo," I pointed out. "Hold up the tent."

"The tent won't be the same without you," Julie replied.

Ren

I had completely hated college. All that studying was not my scene. But things at home weren't turning out to be all that great either.

For instance, I was munching on a Krispy Kreme, when I breezed into my living room that afternoon. My donut eating was completely disrupted by my mother and my little sister, Julie, who were in the middle of a big blowup. Julie's friend, Hannah, was there, too.

"Mom — *hello* — I'm fourteen, not four!" Julie cried.

I immediately saw the cause of Julie's distress. Mom held a PARTY PLAYHOUSE shopping bag. "I just thought your party should have a theme like they used to," she said. "So I stopped on the way home and bought all the stuff."

"Stuff? What stuff?" Julie asked cautiously. From her expression I sensed panic.

Then, to Julie's total horror, Mom reached into the bag and pulled out a big, red, ladybug piñata, ladybug coin purses, ladybug socks, and ladybug headbands with antennas on springs. Mom put on one of the headbands. The antennae boinged and sproinged over her head. "Aren't these antenna boppers so fun?" she asked Hannah.

I thought it might help if I changed the subject, so I spoke up and told them my bad news. "Someone stole my bike," I said. It was true. I'd been in the store buying my donut and when I came out — no bike.

They all stared at me, obviously rendered speechless by my sad tale. I couldn't think of anything else to say, so I moved off into the dining room to finish my donut. They started talking as if I couldn't hear them anymore, but I could hear them just fine.

"What happened to his car?" Hannah asked.

"Repossessed," Julie informed her. "We're all so proud." She made it sound like it was my fault that I couldn't make the last few payments on the car. Getting money is tough when a person doesn't have a job. Somehow jobs never seemed to work out too well for me.

"Maybe I'll just stay home tonight," I heard Mom say.

This threw Julie into *total* panic. "What?! No! Bad! Mom, you can't," she pleaded.

They forgot about me after that and Mom went over the rules for the slumber party with Julie. No boys. No leaving the house. No damaging . . . anything. If she broke any of the rules she'd have to stay home with Grandma and help her sort out her many wigs while the rest of us took our upcoming vacation to Hawaii.

"Are you serious?" Julie cried. She pointed at me in the dining room, jabbing her finger in a way I didn't particularly appreciate. "You would take that . . . *him* . . . and leave *me*? That . . . who is *supposed* to be in college, setting a good example for his younger sister."

I wasn't going to just sit there and take that. "Yeah, well . . ." I said. Then I had to pause to chew the rest of my donut. "College," I went on after I swallowed. "Everyone was so . . . serious. High school rocked. Stay as long as you can."

Julie turned to Mom, her eyes all bugged out. "Please," she pleaded. "Please tell me we have different fathers."

"Enough," Mom commanded firmly. "Go to your room." Then she turned to me. "Ren, you go to your room, too. Go to your former room."

Julie stormed up to her room with Hannah. I went up, too. Being home was so weird. The least they could have done was leave my room alone until they were absolutely positive I was staying at school. Instead, they paneled it and made it like, a yoga and craft center!

Being home was going to be dull . . . dull . . . dull . . .

Julie

I thought Mom would never leave. But, finally, she did. Her girlfriends arrived to pick her up and she drove off with them. "Go! Be merry!" I called, waving from the front door.

She'd left Dad in charge. He was working on installing an Aquapure water filtration system in the kitchen, and that meant he'd pay absolutely no attention to us at all. It was nearly as good as having the whole house to ourselves.

Hannah and I had plenty to do to prepare for the party. I pulled out my best CDs. We played "Get This Party Started" by Pink to get into the party mood.

Farrah arrived first at six and Yancy got there by six-thirty. We had a blast right from the start. We started by swapping clothes and CDs.

Next we did a makeover session. Yancy slapped on all this InstaTan stuff that she'd bought at the dollar store. I tried to make up my eyes to look like Kate Hudson. I wound up looking more like a raccoon than like Kate.

I was ordering two large pizzas, one with anchovies because Farrah insists on eating the stinky little fish, when the doorbell rang. "It had better not be *SpongeBob*," I said as we all ran to the top of the stairs. I didn't know if Russell and his pals really planned to show up, but I was ready to toss them right out if they did.

I hurried downstairs and peeked through the side window. It wasn't Russell. It was even worse — if such a thing was possible.

Our neighborhood is patrolled by a private security company called PatrolTec. One of the guards was at the door, a serious-faced, very official-seeming guy I'd never seen before.

"Who's responsible for this *sound*?" he asked the moment I opened the door.

His shirt had the name SHERMAN stitched over the pocket. "You're not our usual rent-a-cop," I said.

"Chuck had a breakdown," he replied. "This whole zip code is now my domain. And I've got your number, little missy." This guy really thought he was some hot shot. "I got a call about the excessive noise," he mentioned again.

It had to be Mom. Who else could it have been? She'd probably just assumed we'd be making too much noise so she phoned in a complaint ahead of time.

From upstairs, the music from my CD blared. "Turn it down," he insisted.

"Okay, okay," I replied. "Jeez. Bye."

"Turn it up!" Hannah shouted as soon as I shut the door. Farrah ran into my room and cranked up the volume.

The doorbell rang again. I rolled my eyes and sighed.

Sherman was getting to be a real pain. I pulled open the door prepared to tell him that we were just four girls trying to have a little fun.

But it wasn't Sherman. And when I saw who it *was* my jaw dropped open.

Staci

I couldn't believe I was standing on Julie Corky's front doorstep. The evening had started off so well, too.

I'd dressed to kill in my new Kate Spade outfit. After all, I was going to the last high school dance of the year with Todd, Abbott High's star quarterback.

At least that's what *I* thought I'd be doing that night. What I didn't know was that Todd had something entirely different on *his* mind. He picked me up, but he didn't drive us to the dance. Instead, he drove to a secluded spot where he wanted to have a major makeout session.

"Forget that!" I told him. "I spent all month getting ready for this dance and I am going!"

Then, guess what that creep did! He broke up with me, told me to get out of the car, and drove away!

I was furious! But there was no way I was going to sit around and cry. I knew that my friends Liz, Molly, and Jenna were all hanging by the phone waiting to hear from me. I'd said that I'd sneak them into the dance once I got there. That plan was blown, but I'd come up with a new, better one. I immediately called Liz on my cell and told her to start making a list. I'd explain the rest later.

So, there I was on Julie's doorstep, putting step one of

my plan into action. As she opened the door she stared at me in total amazement. I needed to tell a little white lie to explain what I was doing there. "Todd and I had our own private party and then, after that, the dance just seemed redundant, so we decided to take a pass," I said.

"Great," Julie said with an uncertain smile.

I followed her up to her bedroom, which was a shambles. I could see that they'd already done the basic sleepover stuff; the makeover, the clothing and CD swap. "So, let's get this gala started!" I shouted.

I phoned Liz on my cell again. She'd made the list and I told her to send it to Julie's e-mail address. Then I turned on Julie's computer and explained to them what I had in mind. "Liz is having a party of her own," I said as I plopped into the desk chair in front of the computer. "So we decided to put together a little hunt."

Julie and Hannah exchanged this weird look, like they weren't sure if they liked the idea. I checked to see how the other girls were reacting and noticed this pudgy girl I didn't recognize. "Who are *you*?" I asked.

She got all flustered. "Yancy. I'm Yancy. We had PE together all year," she replied nervously.

"You're orange," I pointed out. "You used too much InstaTan!"

Yancy jumped up and looked at herself in the mirror. She seemed about to cry as she rushed out of the room.

"Switch on your webcam," I told Julie. I noticed then that she had a yearbook picture of a high school guy taped to her computer monitor. And she had drawn a heart around it. "Steve Phillips," I said to her. "Dream on." How could she really think she had a chance with a hottie like Steve? Poor, deluded girl.

She just frowned at me and turned on the web cam. Liz, Jenna, and Molly appeared on the screen. "Did you get the hunt list?" Liz asked.

"Opening now," I reported.

"Hunting what?" Julie wanted to know.

"Scavenger hunting," I told her. "Do you have one of those Polaroid sticker cameras?"

"But of course," Hannah said, pulling the Polaroid from her overnight bag.

"Use it to document the tasks," I told her as I printed two copies of the list and handed one of them to her. "We start at eight, sharp as nails."

Liz's voice came from the computer and I turned to look at her on the screen. "We put in something extra special for Julie," she said.

"What?" Julie asked, sounding worried. "What something special?"

Hannah read the list to the group. "Dress a window mannequin at the mall. Get a guy from DatesSafe.com to buy you a drink at the Cosmo Club. Take a security decal off a PatrolTec car. And —"

Julie had been looking over Hannah's shoulder, reading along. Her eyes nearly bugged out of her head when she saw the last task. "Borrow a pair of Steve Phillips's boxer shorts!" she shrieked.

If Hannah hadn't grabbed her, I think she might have actually hit the floor.

What a hoot! I had to hand it to Liz, including Steve's boxer shorts was a stroke of genius.

"No, no, no . . ." Julie murmured.

"What's in it for us?" Hannah asked me.

I hadn't thought about that. "What do you have in mind?" I asked.

"Let's make it interesting," Hannah said as a sly look came over her face. "The lunch spot."

I was impressed. That was bold. "You're on," I agreed.

Hannah grinned. "The winning group gets the spot by the high school fountain next year."

"Ah, I don't know," Liz spoke up.

"And losers eat by the dumpsters," Hannah went on.

"No prob," I told her. This little wager made the whole thing way more interesting. Besides, what chance of winning did these dweebs have against me and my friends? None — and I guess Julie knew it, too. She dragged Hannah out of the room for a discussion.

Hah! This was going to be great!

Julie

"I cannot do the things on that list!" I told Hannah once I had pulled her out into the hall and we were alone. "I'll eat Wonder Bread by the dumpsters with the rest of the frumps."

"Julie, focus," Hannah replied firmly. "What do you want more than anything in this world?" she asked.

That was easy. "Steve," I answered.

"Exactly!" Hannah cried. "Do you think Steve eats by the dumpsters? You could be sitting *right next* to him at the fountain. Plus, if you *don't* do this, *everyone* will hear about it. We live in a sucky universe where wearing the wrong sneakers can make us life outcasts."

"But . . . but," I stammered.

"You and I both know we aren't just talking about a lunch spot," Hannah went on. "You *have* to do this!"

I threw my arms out at my sides and sighed deeply. "I hate when you sound right," I said. "But, we can't leave the house. My mom will cancel Hawaii and, less importantly, my life."

A loud crash came from Ren's bedroom across the hall. Hannah and I each poked our head in and found Ren lying on the floor. He'd fallen off the small cot that was now his bed. After he'd left for college they'd taken out his old bed. When he came back, the little cot was all that was left for him to sleep on.

Hannah looked around, amazed. "What happened to your room?"

Ren got up and brushed his pants off. "Is it different? I hadn't noticed," he joked sarcastically. He gestured around at the wood paneling, the loveseat, the craft desk, and the yoga stuff. He kicked the cot and it folded in half. "And they've eliminated my bed."

"Mom re-did it," I explained to Hannah. "They weren't expecting him back so soon."

"My glory days have been erased!" Ren complained, "my beer cap collection and my cheerleader hate mail — all gone. Now it's a craft corner and a yoga zone. My —"

"Getting back to the real world," I interrupted him.

"We have a proposition for you, Ren," Hannah told him.

I had a good idea of what Hannah had in mind, so I jumped right in. "It involves money," I told him, "my money."

"Your money is my favorite word," he said — as if I didn't know that. "Speak," he went on eagerly.

"Okay," Hannah began, "this is what we're going to need you to do . . ." He listened intently as she told him her plan.

Ten minutes later we returned to my bedroom. Yancy had scrubbed her face and wasn't quite as horrendously orange. Farrah was flipping through magazines and Staci typed on my computer keyboard. "I had to promise Ren fifty dollars to cover for us," I told them.

Staci didn't even look away from the computer. I gazed at it over her shoulder and saw that she was on a website called DatesSafe.com and she was filling in the online application form.

"Wait a minute," I said. I wasn't exactly sure why, but this was making me very nervous. I was sure the DatesSafe.com people wouldn't be too happy about it if they knew a bunch of eighth grade girls were applying for dates on their website.

"She's getting us a neato date for tonight!" Yancy said enthusiastically, as though she actually thought this was a *good* idea.

Stacy rolled her eyes. "Neato?" she scoffed. "Pull yourself into the century." She checked over the application. "Okay, I've told them our name is June and we're twenty-five."

She'd gotten to the line in the application where they asked what her occupation was. "Swimsuit model," she decided, and typed it in. "We're brunette," she said. "And tall. Our hobbies?"

"Dancing," Hannah suggested.

"Sewing," Farrah offered.

"Eating cheese," I added sarcastically. Everyone stared at me like I was crazy. "Kidding," I told them.

"Sitting on the beach," Staci decided and typed it in.

"I'll be wearing . . ." She looked around my room and spotted a purple scarf of mine. ". . . a purple scarf," she said, and typed it in. In the next second she hit SEND.

"And how exactly are you going to be a tall, brunette, twenty-five-year-old swimsuit model?" I challenged her.

"I'm not," she answered. "You are. We'll fix you up."

"Me?" I asked, my jaw dropping.

Suddenly the computer screen changed. "The net rocks!" Staci cheered. "We have a winner!"

"What?" I cried with a gasp. "Already?" I stared at the screen, frantically reading the words printed there. "Dave. Thirty. Handsome. A doctor. Hobbies: reading, hiking, sunsets, and cliff diving."

"He's perfect!" Staci announced and then took over the reading from me. "He'll be wearing a brown jacket and a red tie."

"What does that blue ribbon icon next to his name mean?" Yancy asked.

"It means that he's been verified by the site," Staci explained. "He's all right."

I still wasn't sure about this. I had an absolute rule about not meeting anyone I'd met online.

"And, plus, we're all sticking together, right?" Farrah added.

"Of course!" Hannah agreed. I sighed. I supposed that as long as we all stayed together and were in a public place, it would be okay.

Staci started typing in a reply. She asked him to meet June at the Cosmo Club at nine o'clock.

Just as she e-mailed her message to Dave, the walkie-talkie function on Staci's Boost Mobile Phone came alive. "Honk! Honk! Outside, got the Beemer," we heard Liz's voice speaking.

"Coming," Staci answered as she started climbing out my bedroom window onto the vine-covered trellis outside!

I couldn't believe it! "Where are you going?" I asked, completely stunned.

"You didn't for serious think I was going to be on *your* team, did you?" she asked. I looked at Yancy, Farrah, and Hannah — they looked just as blown away as I felt. "First team to complete all the tasks, documenting them, and then showing at the high school parking lot, wins the fountain spot."

I hung out the window and called down to her. "But we don't have a car," I said.

She smiled up at me as she dropped down onto the porch roof. "Then, you lose," she said. Easily jumping to the railing and then lowering herself to the ground, she ran off toward Liz's BMW at the curb.

I stared at Hannah accusingly. She was the one who had accepted Staci's stupid dare. Now we were stuck going on this insane scavenger hunt. "I blame you!" I said.

But I'd seen that look in her dark eyes before. It was her determined, nothing-is-going-to-stop-us look. "Come on," she said. "We have to turn you into a twenty-five-year-old swimsuit model. Let's go into your mother's closet and see what we can find to dress you in."

Hannah

I rummaged through Mrs. Corky's closet looking for a grown-up, sophisticated dress for Julie to wear. It was pretty hopeless. Finally, though, tucked in the back, I found this incredibly sparkly red dress. It was pretty eighties — which was probably the last time Mrs. Corky had actually worn it — but it was the only thing in there that didn't scream "Mom Outfit!"

Julie put on the dress. Then I piled her hair on top of her head and applied a heavy coat of eyeshadow, blush, and lipstick to her face. "Oh. My. God!" she squealed. "I look like my mother!"

Farrah amazed me by jumping up from the bed and ripping the flower off the dress. She found scissors on the dresser and cut the seam midway on both sides of the sleeves. "I'm not seeing this!" Julie shrieked.

I suddenly remembered that Farrah likes to sew her own clothing and usually looks pretty cute, in a retro, hippie-chick kind of way. She found a sewing box on the floor of the closet and got to work. She tied a ribbon around Julie's waist. "*Now* you look like your mother — twenty years ago, with fashion sense," she announced.

"I think I can get us a car," Yancy said unexpectedly.

I wondered how she'd be able to do *that*.

We went back to Julie's room where Farrah collected some supplies we might need. "Let's go," she announced as she zipped the carryall bag.

Without another word, we hurried back to Julie's room and began climbing out the same window Staci had exited from. Farrah and Yancy made it to the ground first. I was halfway down the pear tree when I noticed that Julie was no longer behind me.

"I'm pretty stuck," she told me in a loud whisper.

I looked up and could see that her heel was jammed into one of the trellis slats.

"Don't be such a lame snack!" I whispered back. "Pull!"

She yanked on the shoe and the next thing I heard was a horrible CRACK! Her shoe heel was still stuck in the trellis but the entire thing had now broken and was hanging right in front of the Corkys' kitchen window.

Julie was now upside down — dress around her ears — dangling like a circus toy in front of the window! I ran over to her beside her. Inside we could see Mr. Corky. He was reading a sheet of directions. We were sure he'd see us any second. But, miraculously, he just kept reading.

Farrah and I pulled at Julie's shoe as hard as we could. And with a *pop*, it came out of the wooden slat . . . and Julie fell, headfirst, onto the ground. "Great rescue, guys," she said sarcastically as she rubbed her head.

"Let's jam," I suggested.

"Where to?" Julie asked.

I looked at Yancy. "Where's this car you can get for us?"

"Come on," she said. "I'll show you." We followed her down several blocks and around a corner until we came to her father's house. She waved for us to follow her into the garage.

Inside, she clicked on the light and there sat a very small car. I mean, really, really small. "Officially the smallest car I've ever seen," Julie remarked.

"It looks like a clown car," I said.

"It's an electric car," Yancy explained. "It's made out of this really hard recycled plastic."

"Way to be environmental," Farrah said, impressed.

"What's with the steering wheel?" Julie asked. "It's slightly on the wrong side."

"It's European," Yancy explained and I remembered that in Europe most cars were built like that. I'd seen it in a British movie once.

"Does it drive?" I asked.

"Oh, definitely. My dad taught me to drive it in the Wal-Mart parking lot," Yancy told us. "He said I could use it in an emergency — which it kind of seems like this is."

"Can we all fit?" Julie asked. To find out, the four of us climbed in from the open hatch door in back. The car only had two seats, so it wasn't exactly comfortable inside.

For a moment it looked as if Yancy wouldn't even be able to shut the hatch door. "Crowd, hold your breath!" she ordered. "One! Two! Three!" With a good strong slam, she got the door to shut. Then she climbed into the driver's seat and started the car!

I couldn't believe we'd even gotten this far — we were definitely on our way, heading to what could be the greatest adventure ever.

Russell

"Destination hottie house ahead," I spoke into my walkie-talkie headset. I coasted down the block on my board, heading straight for Julie's house. This was one sleepover party the girls wouldn't forget, not with me and my boys dropping in on our skateboards to keep the party rockin'.

I glanced over my shoulder, looking for Lance and Miles. I didn't see them. Why couldn't Lance and Miles ever keep up with me on their skateboards?

WHAAAA! I hit a sprinklerhead on the edge of Julie's lawn. My board shot into the air. It went one way and I went the other. But we both landed side-by-side on the lawn. I couldn't let this little setback ruin our plans. "Time for the diary raid," I spoke into my headset.

Lance and Miles heard me without any problem. That may have been because they were standing right behind me. We all picked up our skateboards and headed for the trellis at the side of Julie's house. There was a light on in one of the upstairs windows, so I started climbing toward it. I must say, someone had seriously damaged the trellis, but we managed anyway.

It didn't take long before we were crashing into the room. But where were the girls? The only one there was Ren, Julie's older brother. He seemed to be grilling Play-Doh steaks and chicken on a George Foreman Lean Mean Play-Doh Grilling Machine. I guess being back at home was making him majorly bored.

He looked up from his Play-Doh grill and didn't seem particularly surprised to see us. "Wrong room," he told us as he flipped a Play-Doh steak.

It was a minor setback. We headed down the hall. It was easy to find Julie's room because it looked like a girl's room. There were clothes and CDs thrown all over the place. Our mission — to find her diary! It was a time honored sleepover party tradition: Boys raid sleepover, boys snag diary. Loads of laughs and fun follow. Plus, the diary owner is desperate to retrieve the diary and makes big promises in order to ensure its return.

We entered the room and began looking for the diary. "All I can find are term papers," Lance complained as he searched her desk.

"And socks," Miles added, disappointed.

I pulled open a dresser drawer. "Cha-ching! I found bras!" I announced. It was almost as good as a diary because Julie would definitely want it back.

Ren stood in the doorway watching us. "Dude," he said, "don't you think something's missing?"

I couldn't think of anyzzzthing. "What?" I asked.

"*The girls!*" Miles said, suddenly realizing what Ren meant.

Right! Of course! "Where are the babes?" I asked.

"Gone," Ren informed us.

"Gone?" Lance cried angrily. "This diary raid skeeves." He was right. What good was getting a diary, or even a bra, if there were no girls there to get upset about it?

"It really skeeves," Lance repeated, and this time he shoved me as he said it. He knocked me off balance and I crashed into Julie's dresser with a *thud!*

"Girls?" a man called up the stairs. It was Julie's dad, Mr. Corky. "Everything all right?"

We all looked at one another with panicked eyes as heavy footsteps started up the staircase. Even Ren was worried. I guess he was supposed to be covering for the girls, who had run out for some reason.

At the same moment, we must have all had the same thought. We looked at a bunch of wigs on Styrofoam head forms that sat in the corner of the room. "Grandma's wigs," Ren said. "Put them on!"

He shut the door and we all knew we'd have to work fast. In just minutes, we were ready. Ren put on a CD, the Spice Girls singing "Tell Me What You Want," and turned it up as loud as it would go.

Mr. Corky knocked on the door? "Julie?" he shouted to be heard over the music. When he peeked into the room, what he saw was four girls dancing with their back to him. At least that's what he thought he was seeing. Of course what he was really seeing was us.

He stood a moment — it felt like a *long* moment — and then finally left. "If you tell anyone about this, I will so injure you," Lance threatened me as he pulled his wig off.

I really wasn't paying attention to him, though. I'd spotted something very interesting. Julie's computer was on and there were words written on the screen. I walked closer to read it. In just a minute I realized what it was. I suddenly understood where the girls had gone. "Looks like we're goin' on a hunt, men," I said as I hit the computer's PRINT button and the printer started to make the list.

Julie

I had to give Yancy credit; she really could drive her father's tiny electric car. Being in a car without an adult felt incredibly cool — smushed, but cool. We must have *looked* kind of cool, too, because a carload of mega-cute guys waved to us while we were stopped at a light. "Hot guys never wave at me," Yancy complained as the light changed and they drove off. "What am I saying," she added. "*No* guys ever wave at me. I'm fat."

"You're not fat!" I told her. "Who told you you're fat?"

"Staci and Liz," she answered.

"I've heard they have scales in their gym locker," Farrah said.

"They do!" Yancy confirmed. "They made me stand on it in front of everyone. It was the worst moment of my life."

"That's hideous!" I cried. I could believe it though. Those girls had a mean streak that was pretty wide.

"Yancy, would you rather eat celery or a brownie?" Hannah asked.

Yancy glanced quickly at Hannah while she turned a corner. "Is that a trick question?" she asked.

"Exactly! The answer is obvious. So you'll just date guys

who also like brownies," Hannah pointed out as Yancy pulled into the mall parking lot.

We hurried toward Bloomingdale's department store inside the mall's entrance. The first thing we noticed was Staci, Liz, Molly, and Jenna running toward us. Staci held up a Polaroid photo. They saw us and motioned toward one of the store's windows facing the center court of the mall.

In the display window, a female mannequin was dressed in the outfit Staci had been wearing in school that day.

Okay, so they'd gotten there first. We were just minutes behind them. We still had an excellent chance. But there was something about the smug, victorious smiles they were wearing that made me worry. "Good luck!" Liz said with a smirk.

"Keep it, we don't need it," Hannah shot back confidently.

We ran into the store. It was nearly closing time and there were only a few people still in the store. We headed for the display window, but when we tried to open the door leading to it, it wouldn't budge. "They locked it!" I cried angrily.

"Of course they did," Hannah said, throwing her arms out at her side.

"There's another display window over there," Farrah said, pointing. We followed her over to it. The door wasn't locked. But when we opened it, our faces fell. The mannequin in the window was male.

"They didn't specify the sex of the mannequin," Hannah reminded us.

"True," I had to admit.

Farrah unzipped the supply bag she carried and took out the clothing she'd brought along for us to dress the mannequin. "I don't think he's going to fit into my tube top and skirt," she said.

"We have to try," Yancy insisted. She took the skirt and top from Farrah and ran into the display window. She began unbuttoning the mannequin's shirt.

I watched her, not quite believing she'd had the nerve to do this. Sometimes people really surprised me, and this was one of those times.

"Come on," Hannah said and we all went into the window and began helping Yancy. It wasn't easy. The mannequin's arm fell off when we tried to take his shirt off. But, little by little, we got his clothes off and began dressing him in Farrah's tube top and skirt.

"Freeze!" a man yelled.

We all froze.

Out of the corner of my eye, I looked back into the store and saw the rent-a-cop security guard from Patrol-Tec — Sherman, the one who had come to the house and told us to turn down the music. I thought he'd been the one who spoke. But he was standing still, also frozen, just outside the entrance to the store.

Then another security guard came along and laughed. "Aha! Got you, Sherman!" he said.

Sherman relaxed, but he looked annoyed. "Hello, Dave," he said in an irritated voice. He was speaking to another PatrolTec guard who worked at the mall.

I jerked my head toward the talking guards and my friends unfroze. Slowly and very quietly, we went back to dressing the mannequin.

"Tough day, Sherman?" I heard Dave ask. "That reminds me, a raccoon got loose in a yard and tripped the motion detector. Isn't that a code red for you guys?"

I smiled a little at the joke. The PatrolTec guards act like they're real crime fighters but they seldom have to face any real danger in the peaceful neighborhoods they patrol.

"No, it isn't a code red," Sherman said stiffly. "I just came down here for a little dinner and then I'm going back on patrol."

Sherman glanced in our direction and we all froze once again.

Sherman turned away from us and we relaxed. Hannah took out her camera and took the picture.

"You okay, Sherm?" Dave asked. "You look tense." Just then Dave's walkie-talkie crackled on. "I'll be right there," he answered the person on the other end.

Dave hurried away and I hoped Sherman would leave, too. Instead, he spun around and stared at us. He'd been so fast we hadn't expected him and we didn't freeze. "Hey!" Sherman shouted at us.

He ran into the store but we ran from him. On the way out, I grabbed a mannequin leg that had fallen off. I was the last one out of the display, with Sherman right behind. I slammed the door shut and jammed the leg under the doorknob to make sure Sherman couldn't get out and catch us.

We raced out of the mall to the car. I checked over my shoulder and saw Sherman banging on the window of the display case. His only company was a male mannequin dressed in a skirt and tube top.

"Did that really just happen?" I asked, laughing.

Yancy started up the car. She backed out of her parking spot and peeled away from the lot. She was laughing so hard, she could barely drive. We all were. "I hope they don't sell my clothes," Farrah said between bursts of laughter.

My smile slowly faded as something occurred to me. Hannah noticed the change in my expression. "What?" she asked.

"I just remembered — the pizzas!" I told her. Before Staci had showed up I'd ordered three pizzas. They might have arrived already, and if they had, and Dad had brought them upstairs, we were so busted.

Ren

I heard the doorbell ring and figured: It's not for me. So I kept grilling my Play-Doh food and scratching our dog. Then a little alarm went off in my head. What if it was for Julie and her pals? If Dad went into her room, he'd know that they weren't actually in the house.

Bolting out of my room, I stopped short at the top of the stairs and looked down. Dad stood at the front door, paying for three pizzas. Julie must have ordered them before she and her pals left, and then forgotten all about it. And they say *I'm* the brain-dead one in this family!

Well, I'd promised to cover for them, and I was getting paid to do it, so I had to think of some way to wrestle those pizzas away from Dad. "Dad, I'll deliver those pies to them," I offered, stopping him on the stairs.

"You're going to deliver pizza to your sister?" he questioned. True, it wasn't my usual style to be so helpful.

He looked at me suspiciously and started to walk up the stairs, so I stepped in front of him, blocking his way. "Dad, you have Aquapure momentum," I said. "Don't stop now."

"Good point," he agreed, handing me the pizzas.

Yes! Success! Plus I'd just scored some pizza!

Dad suddenly stopped on his way down the stairs. "In fact," he said to me. "Come and be the first to try the new water."

"So, you're done?" I asked, putting the pizza down at the top of the stairs.

"Yep, just have to tighten the hose," Dad said.

As much as I hated to leave pizzas behind, I wanted to keep Dad from going upstairs. I figured that if I stayed with him, I could at least keep an eye on him.

As we went into the kitchen, the phone rang. Quick as lightning, I snapped it up; worried that it might be Julie. "Yeah?"

"Did the pizzas come?" Julie asked frantically.

I lowered my voice. "My sources say yes," I told her.

"You *have* to make them disappear!" she hissed over the phone. Man, was she ever panicked!

In fact, I'd say she sounded desperate. This was my opportunity for serious negotiating, "What's the offer?" I asked.

"Laundry," she said.

"Keep talking," I countered. I knew she could do better than that.

But she held firm. "Your laundry," she insisted. "I will do your laundry for a month."

"Done," I agreed, hanging up. A month of laundry was pretty good. I never knew Julie drove such a hard bargain.

"Business deal?" Dad asked.

"Exactly," I told him.

"Good for you," he said. He turned on the faucet to pour me a glass of water. "Get ready for some superior tasting water," he said. Some kind of unspeakably grimy sludge began oozing from the faucet. "You go first," I said, waving away the glass of nasty water he was offering me.

For the first time, Dad noticed what was in the glass. He made a disgusted face. "I'd better clean the line," he commented.

Like . . . yeah. "Good thought," I replied.

Dad squeezed himself back under the sink and got to work. "I'm turning off the house water," he said. "Don't flush."

It was a good thing Julie and her pals weren't here for this! And thinking of them not being here reminded me that I was now in possession of their pizzas.

I hurried up the stairs and opened the first box. "Ew! Nasty!" I said when I saw those little dead fish anchovy all over the top of the pizza. I took the pizza and scraped them into the toilet. When I flushed, nothing happened. They just floated there.

Trying not to think about *that* gross image, I went back to my room to consider my next move. The dog trotted in and, together, we stared at the pizzas. "We could throw them all out," I said to him.

The dog gazed up at me with disappointed eyes. But was he the master or was I? It was up to me to show common sense in this matter. "We are not going to eat all this until we're sick," I said.

The dog stared at the pizza. I did, too. How could we let all this delicious pizza go to waste?

We both got into position. "Go!" I shouted and we dove into the pizzas, each of us stuffing our face as fast as we could! Too bad Julie and her buds were missing all the fun here at the house. For a moment, I stopped to wonder what they actually *were* doing at this moment, but then I forgot about them and went back to eating.

Hannah

Yancy pulled into the full parking lot of the Cosmo Club.

"Check it," Farrah said, pointing over to the entrance of the club. Staci, Liz, Jenna, and Molly were sweet-talking the fairly huge bouncer into letting them enter. We watched as they moved past the velvet ropes in front of the Cosmo Club and disappeared inside.

"Come on," I said, squeezing out of the car. I was the first to get to the front door with my friends right behind me. "We're with them," I told the bouncer, "the girls you just let in."

"Yeah with them," someone added from behind us — a familiar, male someone. Together we turned and found Russell, Lance, and Miles standing there.

"*What* are you doing here?" Julie cried.

Russell grinned at us in that annoying way — so unique to Russell. "Scavenger hunting," he said.

"Okay . . . *no!*" Julie told him.

I guess the bouncer had heard about all he could take. "Get gone, all of you!" he growled at us.

"That's so not fair," Farrah protested.

He shot her a nasty smile. "I don't have to be fair," he

43

snarled. "I have the pretty rope." As he spoke, he drew the end of the rope across the entrance, blocking our path in.

There was nothing more we could do there, so we all went back to the car and sat on the curb, considering our next move. It made me so angry that they'd gotten past that bouncer and we hadn't. "I bet your date is inside right now buying Staci a drink," I grumbled.

Russell stared at Julie. "Date? You have a date?" he asked.

"With a doctor," she added.

As we sat there, feeling pretty pathetic and hopeless, a van pulled up. The doors swung open and the band members began unloading their instruments, speakers, and amplifiers. They entered the side door and didn't return, but their helpers came back to get more equipment.

I suddenly had an idea. It was pretty crazy, but we were desperate. When the helpers went back inside, I told my friends to empty the biggest box. Then Julie and I climbed inside. We were squished, but not that much more than we were in Yancy's dad's car.

"I didn't remember this much stuff being here," one of the helpers said when he came back. The other just grunted as they lifted our box onto a dolly. We were bumped and banged, but soon I could hear music playing and knew we were in.

The minute we stopped moving, we pushed the top off

the box and stood up. "That was . . . what was it? . . . oh, yeah, terrible!" Julie said.

"Let's go find your date," I suggested, grabbing her hand and pulling her into the loud club.

What a scene! Neon lights flashed on the dance floor and other lights swirled all over. It was jammed with wall-to-wall people dancing to the pounding music blaring from the sound system. Julie grinned as she took it all in. "I love being twenty-five!" she shouted. "Look at this place."

"It rocks," I agreed.

Across the dance floor I caught sight of Staci and Liz. They'd already managed to collect a small crowd of guys around them. This wasn't good. Liz had probably connected with someone from DatesSafe.com.

I pointed them out to Julie. "They're about to get their picture! We have to find your date, Dave!"

Julie suddenly looked totally surprised. "Hey, is that *Mr. Corrado*?" she asked, spotting our English teacher on the side of the dance floor.

It sure was! "There are no surprises left in the world," I declared.

"Corrado goes clubbing!" Julie said with a gasp. I understood how she felt. It was just too weird to think of English-loving Mr. Corrado making the dance club scene.

Strange and interesting as this was, we had more important things to think about at the moment. "Okay, focus on finding Dave," I said to Julie. "What's he supposed to be wearing?"

"He said he'd be wearing a brown jacket with a . . ." Julie said, then, suddenly, she turned pale, ". . . red tie."

She'd been standing next to a table and now she sank down under it. Grasping my wrist, she pulled me down beside her. "You're wrong, Hannah," she said, still looking pale and sick. "There is one more surprise left in the world."

I furrowed my forehead at her, not understanding.

"Mr. Corrado is my date!" she explained.

"What?" I cried, totally blown away. I stretched up to peak over the table. She was right! He had on a brown jacket and a red tie!

I ducked back under the table. How dare he lie to us like that! "He said he was a cliff-diving doctor!" I said, outraged at his dishonesty.

"I said I was a swimsuit model," Julie reminded me.

"True," I had to admit. "You can't trust anyone nowadays."

"You have to get us out of here," Julie urged. "If he sees us, he'll report us for sure." Mr. Corrado was a cool teacher, but he was still a teacher. She was right, scavenger hunt or no scavenger hunt, we had to get out of here.

It wasn't that easy, though. The place was packed. We got up from under the table and started to push and squirm our way to the nearest exit. "Excuse us," I mumbled.

"Beep! Beep! Moo! Moo!" Julie said as she followed behind me. She suddenly grabbed my arm and squeezed. "He's seen me," she said with a gasp.

I followed the direction of her panicked gaze and saw Corrado heading right for us. Then I realized what was happening. "He's seen *June*," I said to Julie. He was here to meet June, his swimsuit model date who would be wearing a purple scarf. "Get rid of your scarf!"

Julie ripped the scarf off her neck and threw it in the air behind her. It landed on top of a woman's head. "You dropped this," the woman said, pulling the scarf off and handing it back to Julie.

"No!" Julie cried, waving her hands. "I didn't."

"Yes, you did," the woman insisted, still holding out the scarf. She tossed it to Julie and Julie batted it back. The woman returned it again and they tossed it back and forth like a hot potato. Finally, the woman just walked away, letting the scarf flutter to the ground.

I was so busy watching this flying scarf battle that I hadn't noticed Mr. Corrado getting closer and closer. But when I stopped looking at the scarf and was about to speak to Julie — there he was.

Julie's back was still turned to him. But I was staring right at him. In one more second he would recognize me, so I sank behind a potted plant and tried to disappear. I couldn't help Julie now. She was completely on her own.

Julie

"June?" Mr. Corrado asked. I knew his voice from class and didn't even have to turn around to know it was him.

"Sorry, no," I said, trying to disguise my voice. Still not turning, I rummaged in my purse and found a pair of sunglasses. Fast as I could manage, I put them on.

"You're the only one here with a purple scarf," he pointed out.

"Sorry. Not me," I insisted, looking down at the scarf lying on the floor.

"Okay," he said with a sigh. "I know I might be a disappointment physically . . . but I have great wit," he said.

I was dying! He thought I didn't like him so I was giving him the brush off. I couldn't do that to Mr. Corrado, he was such a nice guy! So I forced myself to turn around and face him.

"Nice to meet you," he said with a smile.

"You, too," I replied. At first, I was amazed that he didn't seem to recognize me. But then I supposed that with the swirling lights and my hair put up and the makeup and the sunglasses; it was possible.

"Would you like a drink?" he offered.

"But of course," I replied, doing my best to sound terribly sophisticated. The only problem was that I'd never had a drink. I couldn't even name one. Just in time I got some text-message advice from Hannah over my cell phone. She sent me the name of a drink and I told Mr. Corrado what I wanted. He ordered two drinks for us.

I still couldn't believe he didn't recognize me! He didn't seem to, though. "So, what's it like being a swimsuit model?" he asked.

Naturally, I had absolutely no clue. But he was waiting for an answer and I had to say *something*. "Um . . . cold," I said.

That cracked him up. He laughed so hard that I started laughing. Then, he stopped and a serious expression came over his face. "Have we met before?" he asked. "Your laugh is so familiar."

Uh-oh! My laugh had jolted his memory. I had to stay calm. "Surely not," I replied in my oh-so-sophisticated voice. "I'm trying out different ones until I find the perfect laugh. What do you think of this one?" The other laugh that came out had a heavy snort-snort-snort at the end. I was pretty sure Mr. Corrado thought I was a lunatic by then. But I was doing the best I could under the circumstances.

The bartender showed up with our drinks. "Here's your drink," he said, but he didn't put it down. "Can I see identification?" he requested.

I really felt like I was cornered. The bartender wanted

I.D. and Corrado was staring at me, trying to remember where he'd heard my laugh before.

"Actually, I left my I.D. in the limo," I said to the bartender. He squinted and shook his head, not going for the limo story. He put the drink down under the bar.

"Julie!" Mr. Corrado shouted, suddenly realizing who I was.

He startled me when he shouted and I tumbled backwards off my bar stool. He knelt down and took the sunglasses from my face. "Hi, there, Mr. Corrado," I said sheepishly, feeling majorly embarrassed.

"A swimsuit model?" he questioned.

"Hey, you said that you were a doctor!" I reminded him.

He suddenly looked pretty embarrassed, himself. "My mother always wanted me to be a doctor," he said. He helped me up and we both looked at each other. "This is so typical," he said. "I either get stood up, or worse. *This* is worse."

"It's a long story," I told him, "but the cheat sheet version is that I'm on a scavenger hunt to save my reputation by winning a lunch spot."

"The fountain spot," Mr. Corrado said.

I was amazed. "How did you know about that?"

"I'm not that old," Mr. Corrado replied. "I went to Abbott High School, too. I never did get to sit at the fountain, though." Thinking about his teenaged years, seemed to make him soften toward me. "Okay, get going," he said.

Part of me wanted to run out of there as fast as I could. But I'd come to accomplish something and I'd gotten much farther than I would have ever expected. I really didn't want to give up if there was any way at all that I could still succeed. "Actually, could you buy me a drink?" I asked. I couldn't believe my nerve, but I kept going. "A soda would fulfill the hunt list."

At that moment, Hannah popped out from behind a curtain at the side of the bar. "But I have to get a picture of it," she said, holding up her camera.

Mr. Corrado almost smiled. "I should have known that you'd be nearby." He turned toward the bartender. "Two ginger ales, please."

When the bartender brought the sodas, Hannah snapped the picture! Yes!

We had a real shot at winning now. I looked around the crowd to see if Staci, Liz, Molly, and Jenna were still there. They were, which meant they hadn't gotten their picture yet. Excellent! We'd gotten our picture and the other team still didn't have one. I turned back to Mr. Corrado and Hannah. She was advising him on how to look a little more like a babe-magnet than his usual nerdy self.

Her advice *had* improved him. He'd loosened his tie, mussed his hair, and removed his glasses. He checked his new look in the mirror and smiled. "Who would have guessed?" he said, obviously pleased by the result.

Mr. Corrado asked a woman to dance and she accepted. I watched him move onto the dance floor with her. "Look at all those women out there," I said to Hannah. "They're dancing, flirting . . . *kissing.* Clearly, they all know some vital secret that I don't."

"They're all just pretending, like us," Hannah replied.

I didn't believe it. "Hannah, I spent the last school dance collecting tickets at the door," I reminded her. "I have no real chance with Steve in this life. And we both know it. I'm an adolescent impostor."

As I spoke I noticed some older women moving out on the dance floor. Some of them climbed up onto dance platforms and started rocking out.

"All right!" the D.J. cheered. "Older babe-age shaking their groove things."

Then I saw something I couldn't believe. I staggered backward and gripped Hannah's arm. "I think I just had a stroke," I told her. "Look! Out on the dance floor on one of those little platform things."

Hannah's eyes widened as she saw what I saw. "Is that . . ."

I nodded. "My mother! I can't believe it. She uses Saran Wrap. She makes Mac and cheese and drives a Volvo! She's not supposed to wiggle like that."

"Sometimes even Mac and cheese moms need to shake it a little," Hannah commented.

It was easy for her to be cool about this. It wasn't her

mother out there. "This is terrible," I wailed. "Do you think my dad knows about this? I mean . . . who *is* she?"

"Whoever she is, she's headed this way," Hannah pointed out.

It was true! She'd climbed down from the platform and was walking across the dance floor — heading straight for me. And then she stopped — stopped and bent to pick up the purple scarf I'd dropped on the floor. She turned it over in her hand, studying it. Did she realize it was mine? I couldn't hang around to find out!

Yancy

Hannah and Julie were still inside the club. Russell and his geeky friends had managed to sneak in when the guys from the band left the side door open for a few minutes. That left Farrah and me sitting outside on the curb doing nothing.

Farrah sighed and stood up. "I'm going to go get coffee," she said. "Want one?"

"Nah," I replied. I sat there a few more minutes when one of the helpers from the band came back out. He was cute and looked like he was about seventeen.

"Hey," he said to me. I stood up, assuming he was going to tell me I couldn't hang out there. "You want to sneak in?" he asked instead.

He was actually being nice to me! Guys usually just look through me like I'm not there at all. I'd wanted to go inside, but now I didn't. I preferred standing there and talking to him much more. "No thanks," I said. "I'm waiting for someone."

"Your boyfriend?" he asked.

I nearly burst out laughing. "My boyfriend?" I gasped. Wow! He really thought I might have a boyfriend. "No, I don't have a boyfriend," I told him.

"Are you playing hard to get?" he asked.

Me? Was he kidding? "I'm just hanging out here," I said. "I'm not playing anything."

He nodded and then went back into the club, returning with some more boxes. "I've got to go to another gig," he told me as he started loading the boxes into the back of the van. "Their speakers blew. That's what I do during the summer, I move speakers. It's not like my life goal or anything. But hey, it's money."

"That's nice," I commented. It was lame, I know, but it was all I could think of to say. I wasn't used to cute boys talking to me. He wasn't a total hottie or anything. Still, I liked the way he looked. But it didn't make sense to me. Guys never talked to me. They asked me to hold the door for them sometimes, but that was about it.

"What's your name?" he asked.

"Yancy," I replied.

He stuck out his hand to shake. "Peter," he introduced himself. I shook it and we just stood there smiling at each other. It was really nice. Then he got into his van and drove away.

I was still watching him drive out of the parking lot when Farrah returned with her coffee. "What's with your face?" she asked me. "Your face is all . . . red and funny."

I grabbed her arm excitedly. "A guy!" I told her. "A cute guy — he talked to me! Like a guy talks to a girl that he maybe might like."

Farrah smiled. I guess she could see how awesome meeting Peter had me feel. "Where'd he go?" she asked.

"He left," I replied. And as soon as I said the words, I realized it was true. The total, horrible reality hit me. "I'll probably never, ever see him again," I wailed. "This is the worst night of my life!"

At that moment, Staci, Liz, Molly, and Jenna came out the side door of the club laughing about something they seemed to think was hysterical. "Your girls are in there drinking with *Mr. Corrado*!" Liz told us between bursts of laughter.

"Total grode!" Jenna cried.

"Pa-thet-ic!" Staci added as they ran off to their car.

I turned to Farrah, not quite believing what I'd just heard. "Do you think that could possibly be true?" I asked her.

"Jeez, I hope not," she replied. "He barely passed me."

We didn't have to wait long for our answer. Julie and Hannah came bursting out the back door looking as if they'd just seen a ghost. "My mother's inside!" Julie cried.

"Your mother?" I asked. And I had thought it was weird that Mr. Corrado was in there! Mrs. Corky being in there was beyond bizarre.

Julie and Hannah nodded. "I guess she and her friends do more than eat frozen pies," Hannah remarked.

Julie looked completely stunned.

"I saw her try to call someone. I think she was calling Dad," Julie went on in a panicked voice. "I'm dead!"

"Ren will cover," Hannah suggested hopefully.

"My mom's going to want to talk to me," Julie insisted. We began hurrying toward the car. "I saw that her cell wasn't working inside the club and there was a long line for the pay phone, but Mom is the determined type. She'll get to make that call sooner or later. I have to get home be— fore —" Julie stopped talking as we all stared in horror at Yancy's dad's car. It was totally blocked in by a delivery truck parked behind it.

Julie threw her arms up in frustration. "This cannot happen!" she shouted.

Just then, Lance, Miles, and Russell boarded up behind us. "Where to next?" Russell asked.

Julie suddenly grinned at him. "Russell," she said. "You have to lend me your skateboard."

Julie

Ren had taught me how to skateboard when I was little. Eventually I got even better at it than he was. Although I hadn't boarded in a few years, I guess it's like riding a bike — you never forget.

My friends looked shocked and amazed as they watched me glide out of the parking lot on Russell's board. My ride home required all my skateboarding skill. I had to leapfrog a dog on a leash who was about to collide with me and I nearly met up with a moving car in a crosswalk. Luckily, it stopped in time.

As I crossed in front of that car on the skateboard, I thought, for a second, that the driver was Steve. But, I always think I'm seeing Steve. I suppose that's because he's always on my mind, or not far from it. I've learned not to get too excited when I think I see him. It always turns out that I'm wrong.

Finally, I arrived at my house. Through the kitchen window I could see my dad talking on the cordless phone. I just knew he had to be talking to Mom. Sure enough, he left the kitchen and began walking toward the stairs. I'd told my friends she would want to talk to me! I had to move faster than fast!

The trellis I usually use to get into my room had been broken. The tree was too far away and the drainpipe was too dangerous. I was wondering what to do, when Dad walked out the side door talking on the cordless kitchen phone. "Hold on, honey," he said. It was Mom! "They couldn't have . . ."

I heard Mom's voice squawking on the other end. Her voice was high and agitated.

Dad noticed that the trellis was broken. I guess he was going to fix it, because he went into the garage and came back with a ladder, which he leaned against the house. But, before he could step onto it, he looked through the kitchen window and saw Ren. My big brother was about to turn on the faucet. "Don't! Stop!" he yelled. He ran back into the kitchen to stop Ren.

That was my chance! I scrambled up the ladder as fast as I could. Luckily Mom's high heels were still attached to my belt where I'd stuck them.

I got to the porch roof, but tore Mom's dress on the gutter. There was no time to worry about it. If I knew Mom, she'd be demanding to talk to me any second now. Hurrying up the roof, I was nearly at my window when a tile came loose under my foot. I slid all the way back to the edge of the roof. I gripped the gutter just in time to avoid failing off the roof altogether.

Pulling myself up, I hurried back across the roof and hurled myself through the window. Ren was inside my room playing the computer really loud. He was trying to make it sound like we were still in there. "Julie?" my dad was calling from the other side of my closed door. "Julie? Mom wants to talk to you."

I was too out of breath to answer him. I sat on the bed, just trying to breathe. Ren grabbed my robe and threw it over me.

"Hello?" Dad called again, knocking. "Jules?"

"Yeah, Dad?" I said, forcing my voice out. I wiggled into my robe just time.

Dad opened the door a crack and handed the phone to me. "Here," he said. "It's your mom."

I took the phone from him. "Everything okay?" Mom asked.

I tried my best to sound calm and casual. "Of course, Mom, everything's peach."

"You sound out of breath," she commented. I should have known she'd notice. She doesn't miss a thing.

"We were . . . cleaning my room," I lied.

There was silence on the phone. Did she believe my cover up story? Finally, she spoke. "Okay, then, see you later. Bye."

"Bye." I sighed with relief. That had been way too close.

Ren looked like he was about to faint. "I'm freakin' exhausted!" he cried, collapsing onto my bed. "I need to go back to college to get some rest!"

I had to admit it — Ren had really come through for

me tonight. "I don't know how to say this," I told him, "but . . . thanks."

Just then, car headlights flashed into my bedroom. Checking out the window, I saw my friends at the side of the house in Yancy's dad's car. They'd just dropped Russell off to pick up his skateboard, which I'd left outside. I turned back to Ren. "Can you cover just a little longer?" I requested.

"Go! Be a teenager," Ren answered. "It ends too soon and gets replaced by wood paneling." I knew he was talking about his newly paneled bedroom. At that moment I was really glad he was my big brother.

I threw off my robe and climbed back out the window. As soon as I squeezed into the tiny car, Yancy headed for Steve's house. Our next assignments were to score a Patrol-Tec decal and a pair of Steve's boxer shorts.

We pulled up across the street from Steve's house. It probably looked just like a regular house to anyone else, but to me it practically glowed. After all, Steve, the guy I was madly in love with, might be inside. I was busy staring at it lovingly — when the car conked out. "Uh-oh," Yancy murmured as it stopped and went completely dark.

"You ran out of juice in front of his house?" I cried.

"The car has a quick charge function," Yancy said. "I just need a plug."

"A plug!" I yelled. Where on earth were we going to get a plug?

"Calm yourself," Hannah told me. "We'll take care of the car. You go get his boxers."

"Hold up," I said. "Why do I have to boost his boxers?" I thought this was a team effort.

"Are you kidding?" Farrah asked. "The only reason this is even on the list is because of you."

"She's right," Hannah agreed. "This one is all you."

It seemed there was no way I was getting out of this. I was nervous beyond nervous as we all got out of the car and hid behind it, staring at Steve's house. "Do you think he's in there?" I asked.

"It's almost ten," Hannah replied. "He might be at the high school dance by now."

"Or he might be inside getting ready," Farrah suggested. "No one great shows up before ten." Why did she have to say *that*? What if he was actually there and I ran into him? I'd die of embarrassment right on the spot!

Slowly, I rose and walked out from behind the car. I began to cross the street — then abruptly turned back. "Okay, let's go. We lose. I can't do it," I told my friends.

Hannah took a firm hold of my two arms. "You are Julie. Great knees and powerful brain! You can do this!" she said.

"*Great knees*? *Powerful brain*?" I questioned. Was that the best she could come up with?

"Just go do it!" Hannah insisted, turning me around and shoving me lightly.

Terrified, I went across the street toward Steve's house.

I kept to the shadows by the side of the house as I moved down the driveway and tried the back door. Yes! It was unlocked.

As I crept into the dark kitchen, my foot kicked a sneaker — Steve's sneaker! Snapping it up, I hugged it to me. The sneaker of my beloved! And then I saw his skateboard lying on the kitchen table. Goosebumps sprang up all along my arms. Reaching out, I touched it. I knew this was just insane, but it was so wonderful!

I heard voices from another room! Steve's voice! I dropped to my hands and knees and crawled rapidly behind the counter just as Steve walked in with a friend of his named Gregg. Gregg pulled open the refrigerator and light poured out from the bulb inside. My heart pounded as I pulled myself into the tightest ball possible.

They were talking about some girl Steve had seen, a girl he obviously liked. It sounded like he had seen her just a short while ago.

I had to get out of there! Still on hands and knees, I scurried out of the kitchen and down a hallway.

I turned and saw Steve coming right at me except that he was thumbing through an old yearbook. Panicked, I dove into the first room I saw. It was a bathroom. Through a crack in the door, I could see Steve walk by. It seemed that somehow he hadn't noticed me.

"I found my junior high yearbook," he called to Gregg. "You know, I think this is a picture of the girl I saw tonight."

He stopped right outside the door. I heard pages turning. He was probably looking for the lucky girl's photo.

Then I had a worrisome thought. What if he needed to use the bathroom? To be safe, I stepped into the shower and pulled the curtain shut.

"I think I knew her in like junior high or something," Steve told Gregg. I heard Gregg's footsteps as he joined Steve in the hall. Steve began reading the list of clubs the girl belonged to that were listed under her picture. "Drama club, basketball, debate team," he read.

Hey, wait! I thought. I must know her. I belonged to all those clubs in junior high, too.

"Her hobbies are hot dogs, skateboarding, and napping," Steve went on.

Those were the hobbies I had listed in the yearbook! Could they be talking about *me*? It seemed impossible and yet . . .

I leaned forward to hear them better. And suddenly a hand waved in front of my face. It was Steve's. I hadn't even heard him come in!

Steve stood outside the shower, groping around, trying to locate the faucet handle. "Hurry, the dance ends at midnight," Gregg said to him from outside the bathroom.

"Yeah, yeah," Steve shouted back, still feeling for the handle. Finally, he found it. I ducked back, but not fast enough. He turned on the shower and I was right under it. It was hard not to yell as I was completely *soaked* in water. Any second now, Steve was going to pull back the curtain and find me standing there. And all he'd be wearing was . . . what people usually wear when they're about to take a shower.

Then — *smash*! Something out in front of house made a loud crash. "What the hell was that noise!" Steve shouted to Gregg.

"Sweet! It's right out in front of your house. Someone smashed into the PatrolTec guy!" Gregg reported.

Hannah

Yancy, Farrah, and I sat hiding behind a bush across the street and down the block from Steve Phillips's house. I sure hoped Julie was having an easier time inside than we were having out here.

After Julie went into the house, we went looking for a plug so we could recharge the car. We found one on the side of a house just around the corner. We ran back to the car and began pushing it toward the house with the plug.

At first we didn't realize that we were going downhill. But it didn't take long before the car started rolling — and it rolled right into the PatrolTec security guard's car!

The guard jumped out of the car and we ran. It was Sherman, the same guard who had come to the house and who we'd locked in the display window at Bloomingdale's. That guy seemed to be everywhere!

Of course, I didn't think it was exactly a coincidence that he was here right now. I had a strong hunch that Staci and Liz had seen Julie go into Steve's house and had given him a call. I had to hand it to them, it was a clever way to get the decal they needed and bust Julie at the same time.

Sherman hunted around for us, but didn't see that we

were crouching in the bushes behind him. What he did see, though, was Julie running up the side of the house. It was hard to tell in the dark, but I thought she had Steve's boxer shorts in her hand.

As Sherman approached Julie, we came out of the bushes and crept behind Yancy's dad's car to watch. When he shined his big flashlight at Julie, she froze like a terrified deer caught in a car's headlights. "I got a call about a suspicious person at this address and *you* look suspicious to me!" he bellowed at her. He stepped closer, staring hard at her. "Hey, haven't I seen you before?"

Julie looked pretty different from when he'd seen her at her house and at the mall. Plus, she seemed to be soaking wet for some reason. Maybe he wouldn't remember were he'd seen her. I hoped not — because if he did he might recall where she lived, too.

"No, no, I don't think so," Julie told him.

We had to get Julie out of there, but there wasn't much we could do with a conked-out car. Farrah and Yancy must have been thinking the same thing because without even discussing it, the three of us got behind the car and started pushing it toward the plug.

We were lucky in three ways. Sherman was so busy questioning Julie that he didn't notice us, our car wasn't damaged, and it was so tiny that it was easy to push. We were able to push it to the house around the corner and plug in. While we waited for the car to charge, Russell and his posse skated up to us. "Did you already panty-raid skater boy Steve," Russell asked, holding up the hunt list.

"Yeah, but Julie got nabbed by Joe PatrolTec," I told him. "She needs a hero."

Russell grinned at me and I could see that he already had an idea. When he told it to us, I had to give the boy credit — it wasn't totally stupid. And nobody else had any ideas, so we went with Russell's plan.

Once the car was all charged up and running again, Yancy, Farrah, and I drove slowly back to Sherman's car. Yancy had to drive slowly because our car was blocking Sherman from seeing Russell. Russell was lying on his skateboard, keeping low and out of sight.

Luck was with us because Julie was following Sherman into his car just as we got there. Yancy slowed down as I pushed open the door. "Julie!" I shouted to her, "jump in!"

Julie bolted for the car — but then suddenly stopped. "What are you doing?" I cried.

Julie ran back and grabbed the decal from Sherman's car. "Winning!" she shouted as she dove into the car.

"Hey! That's my official decal!" Sherman yelled angrily. I noticed that both decals were gone from the car. The other team had gotten their decal, also, but we were still in the running.

Yancy floored the gas pedal and we took off. Behind us, Sherman tried to follow. He didn't get far, though. As soon as he started up his car, it wobbled badly to the right. "Way to go, Russell!" I cheered. He'd let all the air out of Sherman's tires!

I turned to Julie. "Lunch spot? Who cares?" I asked.

"I do!" she shouted her reply. I hugged her. This was the spunky Julie I remembered from when we were kids, the one I knew was still inside her somewhere.

"I got these boxers by hiding in the shower," Julie told us. "He was about to step inside when something crashed out here."

"That was us hitting the PatrolTec guy's car," Farrah filled her in.

"Oh, well, it was a good thing you did because it distracted Steve so I could escape with the boxers. The PatrolTec guy nabbed me and called my father," Julie recalled, "but luckily Ren picked up the phone and pretended to be him. We have everything. Head for the high school dance."

I wondered how Staci, Liz, Jenna, and Molly were doing. That other missing PatrolTec decal made me nervous. Had they somehow scored a pair of Steve's boxers, too? Were they already at the high school? Were we too late?

Just then we passed a place called Jamba Juice and I spotted Liz's BMW parked outside. I guess they were so confident about winning that they thought they had time to spare.

"They stopped for juicers?" Julie cried, her voice full of disbelief.

"Smug people need lots of hydration," Farrah commented wryly.

The four of them came out of Jamba Juice at that very moment. We stopped at a light and Staci saw us right away. They scrambled into the car and Liz peeled out of the parking lot.

"Drive!" I yelled the moment the light changed. "Drive!"

Julie

Liz and Yancy both pulled to a stop side by side, in front of the high school, at the same moment. I leaped out of the car. "Tie!" I shouted, my arms held high.

Staci sprang out of Liz's car next. "Calm your jets," she said harshly. "Let's compare goods first."

Triumphantly I took out Steve's boxers, the decal, and the pictures of Mr. C. buying me a ginger ale in the club, and of the male mannequin wearing Farrah's clothes at the mall. I placed them on the hood of the car. Standing back, I grinned at Staci, silently daring her to top that!

Staci dumped all her team's items on the hood of Liz's car. My smile drooped a little when I saw that they also had everything they needed. "Where did you get those boxers?" I demanded suspiciously.

"We found them in a gym bag in the backseat of his car parked in the driveway," she revealed.

I had to hand it to them for thinking of that. For a second, both teams stared at all the items we'd collected. "So, all things now being equal," Liz said, "we'll have to do a tie-breaker."

"What? No!" Hannah objected. "We share the spot."

"Share? With you?" Staci scoffed disdainfully. "I don't think so. Tie-breaker — winner takes all!"

"You're on!" I accepted boldly. I didn't know what was happening to me. I was suddenly filled with a new confidence. We'd gone through so much to get this far and we'd gotten past such unbelievable obstacles that it seemed like we could accomplish anything!

"The first one to get the king or queen's crown at the dance wins," Liz suggested.

"What?!" Hannah shrieked. I understood how she felt. How were we supposed to get our hands on *that*?

But before we could object, Jenna interrupted. "Hey, Staci, isn't that Todd's car?" All of us turned and stared at the red convertible parked at the curb.

"That *is* his car," I remarked. "I thought you said you guys decided to skip the dance, Staci."

Staci's face reddened but she just glared at me. It was pretty obvious that something had gone wrong between them and she hadn't told the truth about it. Tossing back her perfect blond hair, she stormed into the dance. Liz, Jenna, and Molly trailed behind her.

If they were going into the dance, so were we! I pulled a small mirror from my purse and wiped up my smudged eye makeup. "Are we really going in?" Yancy asked me.

"You bet we are," I told her. We weren't going to give up now.

I stepped toward Abbott High just as Russell, Miles, and

Lance zoomed up on their boards. "Did you see that rent-a-cop conk out right into that tree?" he gloated.

"Thanks," I said. As much as I hated to admit it, Russell had really come through for us. "I guess I owe you."

"Nah," he said with a wave of his hand. "We're level. Did we win?"

"Almost," I replied. "We have to get the crown."

Russell pulled out the hunt sheet and scanned it quickly. "What crown?"

There was no time to answer him. A crowd of Abbott High students were moving toward the front door of the school. If we were ever going to be able to sneak in, this was our opportunity. I ran up the stairs and tried to act like I belonged there with the high school kids, but a serious-faced high school girl at the door spotted me. She reached out and blocked my path with her arm. "No I.D., no entrance, no way!" she barked.

I faced her and looked at her. She wore baggy clothes. And had an unhappy look in her eyes. "I know who you are," I said to her.

"You . . . do?" she asked, confused.

I nodded. "You're out here collecting tickets instead of being inside at the dance. Your dream guy probably came through and handed you his ticket and you said, 'Hi, Bobby. . .'"

"Scott," she corrected me.

"'Hi, Scott.' And he just grunted and walked by. You've

liked him for the last four years and he never even bothered to learn your name." I could tell from the look on her face that I was getting it right. "You spend weekends doing extra credit algebra," I continued. "And you've never eaten anywhere near the fountain."

The girl nodded sadly.

"In four years I'll be you — *unless I get into that dance!*" I told her.

The girl swung the door wide open. "You go! Get in there!" she said with a grin.

I hugged her gratefully.

"Do it for all those who never could," she cried as my friends and I went in.

We hurried to the gym where the dance was being held.

A banner strung across the dance floor announced the theme: A NIGHT TO REMEMBER. "So this is it, a high school dance," I said to my friends. It was just the way I'd always pictured it would be, with Mylar balloons, papier-mâche palm trees, a bubbling punch fountain, a picture-taking booth, strobe lights, and majorly loud band. It was sure different from the dances at our junior high where they served warm Kool-Aid and made us take off our shoes so we wouldn't scuff the floor.

I looked around for Steve, but only caught sight of Russell, who was already out on the dance floor busting his unique Russell-style moves. "Hey, Spazmonkey, stand still," Hannah snapped at him.

We didn't have time to dance. We had a crown to find. "Let's scope," I advised. I took the lead as we began to circle the outskirts of the dance floor.

I wasn't exactly sure what we were looking for. Maybe it wasn't an actual thing or a person. I suppose we were searching for an opportunity to grab hold of the crown — hoping to be at the right place at the right time.

Hannah tapped me on the shoulder. "Look over there," she said, directing my gaze across the dance floor. Todd, Staci's boyfriend, was standing among the papier-mâché palm trees kissing a girl who was definitely not Staci. And we also saw something they *didn't* see. Staci and her friends were charging toward them angrily. "Major badness," Hannah murmured.

The music stopped and the band's lead singer spoke into the microphone. "We're about to begin the dance contest so grab a partner," he said.

My friends and I rushed over to the palm trees to witness this fight. We got there just as Staci grabbed hold of Todd's arm, yanking him out of the kiss. "I guess you changed your mind about going to the dance!" she shouted at him accusingly.

"Staci!" Todd gasped.

Staci slapped him hard in the face.

"Who the hell are you?" the girl Todd had been kissing demanded.

"I'm his girlfriend!" Staci informed her.

"That's funny," the girl said. "Because I'm Linda his girl-friend and I have been for six months!"

The girl looked older than Staci. She was probably in high school and that was why Todd had been able to keep them apart.

Everyone gasped when Linda shoved Staci. Staci staggered back a few steps then rushed forward and shoved her back. "Me-ow! Hiss! Hiss!" Russell cried, hurrying over and hoping to witness his first cat fight.

The band's singer noticed the fight. "What's that?" he asked, looking in our direction. "A rumble in the jungle?"

Staci and the girl didn't even notice the band's singer. They were now locked in battle, yanking at each other's hair. Staci tore Linda's weave off and, furious, she pushed Staci into one of the trees. Staci bounced off the tree and hit a papier-mâche rock. Her clothes were snagged on a ripped piece of papier-mâche and she couldn't get up again. "Stay away from *my* footballer," Linda warned her.

"You can *have* him!" Staci screamed at her.

"The mojo dance contest will now begin," the band's singer announced.

Liz tried to unhook Staci from the rock as Todd walked away with his other girlfriend. Russell jumped in front of him. "Where are you going?" he demanded.

"Get real, she's not worth it," Todd said scornfully.

"Are you kidding?" Russell cried in disbelief. "Staci?

Staci is a prime goddess! If I had a girl like Staci, I would *worship* her."

Todd just laughed at him. Even though Staci could be pretty mean at times, it seemed that Todd was even meaner. I think everyone there felt sorry for her at that moment.

"You're just dumping her? Typical quarterback move," Hannah spoke up.

"Come on, Todd," his new girlfriend insisted, "let's go command the dance contest." She sneered at Staci, who had gotten free of the rock. "Too bad, so sad, you don't have anyone to enter the contest with."

"Yes, I do!" Staci told her. Everyone was shocked and amazed as she grabbed hold of Russell's hand.

Todd burst out with nasty laughter. "You've got to be kidding!"

"Staci, did you fall on your head?" Jenna asked.

Russell shot her an angry look. "I can dance!" he told Jenna as he moved out onto the dance floor with Staci.

Hannah, Farrah, Yancy, and I looked at one another. "What do you say, girlfriend?" Hannah asked.

"We don't have anyone to dance with," Yancy said.

"The only partners we need are each other," I told her as I headed out onto the dance floor.

All around us, kids were dancing like their life depended on it. And the couple who was really blowing them all away was Russell and Staci. Both of them were flipping in the air while kids nearby applauded. I remembered that Russell was a gymnast and as head cheerleader, Staci was able to match him move for move.

There were two platforms that had been set up for dancing. So far, no one had been brave enough to get up on top and dance on them. Hannah looked at them and then turned to me. "What do you think?" she asked.

"Absolutely!" I told her. I got up on one platform while she climbed onto the other. We both started to rock out. I felt so great — so free! "Freshman year — I have arrived!" I shouted.

Russell

My life was suddenly very good — major good! I was showing off all my best gymnastic moves on the dance floor of Abbott High School and my partner was super-babe, cheerleading captain Staci Holden.

I really, really hoped this wasn't just a dream. But, even if it was, it was one great dream.

Being a cheerleader, and all, Staci could flip and tumble like a champ. High school kids surrounded us, cheering and clapping.

Not far away from us, her ex-boyfriend Todd danced with his date. Boy, were they lame! Actually, the girlfriend wasn't a bad dancer, but Todd was a real stick. For a football player, that guy really didn't move well.

I did an awesome cartwheel and, as I turned, I saw my hunt list fall out of my pocket to the ground. Oh, well, it wasn't like I needed it anymore. The crown was the last thing we had to get. I'd written it in with a ballpoint pen at the bottom of the list, but I wasn't likely to forget what it was.

Staci and I went on dancing. Out of the corner of my eye I saw that guy Julie likes, Steve Phillips. He bent down and picked up the list I'd dropped and read it. His friend poked him and pointed at Julie, who was now rocking out on top of a dance platform. He looked excited to see her. I wondered — did he like Julie as much as she dug him? If it was true, that would work out extremely well.

The song ended and the band singer announced the winner. "There's clearly one shining couple here tonight," he said. He jumped down from the stage and grabbed our hands! Everyone cheered! Well, almost everyone. I noticed Todd and his girlfriend kind of grumbling, but that only made our victory that much sweeter.

A photographer snapped our picture as the band guy handed us a trophy. We smiled at each other and out at the crowd. This would definitely ease my entry into high school next year. Surely *some* kids would remember me as the guy who won the dance contest with an awesome, popular girl as my partner.

The photographer handed me two Polaroid shots of Staci and me with our trophy. That reminded me — "Hey, want to see a picture of me in a coma?" I asked Staci.

"Okay," she agreed.

"Really?" I asked. Girls never wanted to see this picture. Maybe this *was* a dream. But in case it wasn't, I dug into my pocket and pulled out the photo.

"Sweet," Staci said, sounding truly impressed. Then she seemed to remember who she was, and who I was. "You know, this doesn't mean we're boyfriend and girlfriend or anything."

"I know," I told her. The good news was — now I knew it wasn't a dream.

"I mean, it's not like we're going to hang out or anything," she went on.

There was another bright side to all this, too. "I know it doesn't mean we're together now," I said, holding up the Polaroid of Staci and me, "but now I have this picture! And this is way better than my coma picture!"

Miles and Lance rushed up to me. Miles's eyes nearly popped out of his head when he saw the photo. "You are an insta-legend!" he gushed.

"Can we have a picture taken with you?" Lance asked Staci.

"Be cool, guys," I warned them.

Julie and Hannah had jumped down from their platforms. They were joined by Farrah and Yancy, who rushed over to congratulate Staci and me. Even though Staci was on the other team, for this quick moment, we were all together in this victory.

"This is the sweetest slumber party ever!" Yancy shouted.

"Yeah!" Farrah added. "Aren't you glad Staci couldn't come?"

The smile suddenly disappeared from Yancy's face. "What? Why?" she asked.

"Because Julie's mom only let her invite three girls," Farrah blurted out.

People always tell me I'm *not* the most sensitive guy in the world, but even *I* could see that Yancy was crushed by this news. "I was the replacement?" she asked.

"I mean . . . no," Farrah said. She was trying to take it back, but it was too late. Yancy's eyes filled with tears and she ran off.

I'd heard the whole conversation, but Julie hadn't. She only saw Yancy run off, upset. "What did you say to her?" she asked Farrah.

"I told her that she replaced Staci at the party," Farrah admitted.

"Way to be a friend," Julie said.

"I'm sorry," Farrah replied.

"Let's go find her," Julie suggested. She and Farrah ran off together to find Yancy.

As they left, I saw someone had been standing behind Julie — someone she hadn't noticed at all. Steve had been about to tap Julie on the shoulder. It looked like she had just missed her big moment with Mr. Wonderful.

Yancy

I found a spot in the bleachers and sat down, tears streaming down my cheeks. It had been such a great night. I'd really felt like I belonged. And then, learning that I was just an afterthought, a replacement . . . well, it hurt.

It wasn't like I could blame Julie, Hannah, and Farrah. They'd been very cool to me. It was just that I'd never been too popular and when Julie invited me I thought it was because they liked me. Now I discovered I was just filling in a blank spot. I wondered what it was. Why didn't anybody think *I* was special? Okay, I guess I was feeling sorry for myself, but it was how I felt. My new friends probably thought I was a real dweeb for running off the way I had.

Over on the stage, the band's singer returned to the microphone and spoke into it. "Before we announce the king and queen, we have a special dedication," he said.

I listened to who was lucky enough to have someone dedicate a song to him or her. "To Yancy," the singer said.

I blinked hard. Was there another Yancy out there? He couldn't possibly mean me! Could he?

"This song comes out to you from the speaker-moving guy you met at the Cosmo Club tonight," the singer continued.

It *was* for me!

This was unbelievable — unbelievably great! I looked over to the stage and there he was, standing beside an amplifier. Peter, the cute band equipment mover, was staring right at me.

I felt as if I was in a trance as I got up from the bleacher and floated over to him. Somehow my feet got me to where he stood. "What are you doing here?" I asked.

"I told you I had another gig," he explained with the dreamiest smile. "I saw you dancing out there with your friends. Want to try it with a partner?"

Gazing into his eyes, I nodded. "Yes," I said and we left the stage to go down to the dance floor. Together we danced to the song that he'd had dedicated to me. As we held each other close I felt like I was exploding with happiness. He liked *me* as I was, extra pounds and all. I recalled what Hannah had said, about finding a guy who would also like treats. "Do you like brownies?" I asked.

"Are you kidding?" he said. "Brownies are an important food group."

I leaned my head on his shoulder and smiled.

The song ended and I hoped another one would start right up. But, instead, the singer started talking. "And now the moment you've all been waiting for," he announced. "You've been voting all week for king and queen . . ."

This meant the crowns would be coming out!

Julie

I froze when I heard the announcement. Once we saw that Yancy was okay, Hannah, Farrah, and I had sneaked backstage, searching for the crowns. Now, it seemed, we'd run out of time.

We moved to the stage wings where we thought the crowns might be. Liz, Molly, and Jenna were already there. "The crowns aren't here," Liz told us.

"So you haven't won," Hannah reminded her.

"Yet," Liz shot back.

"We're not giving the fountain spot to you dumpster frumpsters," Jenna added.

"Talk, talk, talk . . . no action," I said.

We could see out onto the stage. Hannah touched my elbow as the band singer took his time opening the envelope that held the names of the Abbott High king and queen. "Jennifer Allen and Steve Phillips!" he announced.

Steve had won! I was so excited for him that I forgot all about the contest. He'd won! The greatest, cutest guy I knew had won.

Nearby I heard a cheer and turned toward it. Jenna, Molly, Liz, and Staci had also come backstage looking for crowns. Now they were high-fiving one another triumphantly. Jenna turned in our direction, grinning. "Jennifer is a bud of mine," she explained. "She'll give me the crown for sure."

We were sunk. And I had been so sure we could win!

From one side of the stage, Jenna's friend, Jennifer, ran excitedly to the center of the stage. Steve sauntered on from the other side, cool as ever. He looked as if he wasn't sure if this was a good thing, or just dumb. "Speech! Speech!" his skater friends yelled from the dance floor, but he just waved them off.

The band singer placed a crown on each of their heads. "Choose your partners!" he told them. "This song is reserved for you."

Jennifer found her boyfriend at the side of the stage and led him to the dance floor for the slow song the band was playing. I wondered what lucky girl Steve would want to share this moment with. He peered out into the crowd as if he was looking for someone special. Then he took the microphone and spoke into it. "Julie?"

I stood there gazing at him, in a daydream. In my fantasy, Steve had spoken my name, asking me to dance.

"Julie Corky?" he said again.

"Julie!" Hannah said loudly, pushing me lightly. "He just said your name!"

"What?" I asked her. Was she telling me I wasn't dreaming? "That was real?" I asked.

This time Hannah pushed me hard, right out onto the

stage. My heart rose into my throat as I stood face to face with Steve. "Want to dance?" he asked.

It's pretty hard to talk with your heart pounding in your windpipe — so I just nodded and kind of fell into his arms. He held me close and I realized it was all true.

After a few moments on the dance floor, I was able to speak again. "I didn't even think you knew who I was," I confessed.

He lifted his crown from his head and placed it on mine. "You win," he said.

I snuggled next to him. Oh boy, had I ever won!

I heard wild, victorious shouting coming from nearby. Hannah and Farrah were jumping and cheering. They'd seen me get the crown. They knew we'd won the lunch spot!

I also saw Molly, Jenna, Liz, and Staci scowling at me angrily. They weren't used to losing at anything. This was obviously a big shock for them.

We danced for several more songs. I didn't want this night to end, but finally they announced that the dance was over. Steve took my hand and we walked out the front door. We stopped a moment by the lighted fountain in front of the school. "So, how did you know," I asked him, "about me, and you, and the crown?"

"I saw you earlier tonight, boarding," he said. I couldn't believe it! That moment when I'd thought I saw Steve, I guess it really had been him in the car. "And then when I saw you out there on the platform dancing, it all fit," he added.

"And the crown?" I asked. "How did you know I needed that?"

He pulled the scavenger list from his back pocket. "By the way, can I have my boxers back?" he asked.

I was *so* embarrassed! I laughed nervously and I'm sure my face was red.

"I like your laugh," he said. He leaned close to me and somehow I knew I was about to receive my first kiss. He was so close I could practically feel his lips on mine . . .

. . . and then my cell phone rang!

The magical moment was ruined! "Sorry," I said. "I'd better . . . it might be . . ."

"Go ahead," he said, stepping back.

I wondered if we were busted. Was this Dad or Mom? "Hello?" I answered nervously.

"Where are you tarts?" Ren demanded.

"Does Mom know we're not home?" I asked urgently.

"Mom's not home yet but she's on the way," he reported. "She just called. Get home now!"

Hannah, Farrah, and Yancy must have been watching me because they rushed to my side. "Who was it? Was it your mom?" Hannah asked frantically.

I turned to Steve to explain. "My mom doesn't know we left the house. She's on her way home and if . . ."

"What?" Hannah shrieked. "Let's go!"

"As unbelievable as it is," I said to Steve, "I have to go."

"Oh," he replied, sounding really bummed.

"I'm sorry, I —" Hannah yanked me along and I didn't even get the chance to finish my sentence. I only had time for one last look at Steve as she practically dragged me to Yancy's dad's car.

Yancy pulled up to the house. Mom wasn't there yet but we had one huge problem. Dad had removed the ladder. There was no way into the house.

Then, suddenly, I looked up and saw Ren standing in my bedroom window and it gave me a brilliant idea. "The fort!" I cried. "Follow me." I led my friends over to Ren's old play fort, in a tree near my window. It was near, but not near enough for us to get to the roof. Still . . . there might be a way.

We scrambled up the fort ladder. When we were up in the fort, I grabbed hold of the swing rope that hung down. Waving, I got Ren's attention and he opened the window. "Catch it!" I yelled, tossing the rope to him.

Ren caught it the first time and he tried to stretch the rope from the fort into my bedroom window. I didn't know if it would work, but I couldn't think of anything else. I gripped the rope tightly in my two hands and began to shimmy across to my bedroom.

I was amazed that Ren was able to hold the rope. I saw that he had the dog helping him. But, when I was about midway there, the rope sagged. "Pull it tight!" I yelled.

Ren yanked on the rope. I guess he didn't know his own strength — neither of us did. Because he pulled the entire fort over so that it fell on top of the roof.

The good news was that it was super simple for my friends to climb out onto the porch roof and into my bedroom.

We got in just as Mom's friend's car pulled in the driveway and Mom got out. We dove under the covers. "Assume sleep positions," I hissed just seconds before Dad opened my door a crack.

"Told ya, no problem," Dad told Mom. "Did you have fun at the club?"

"Yes, but I missed you," Mom replied, giving him a peck on the cheek.

"Everyone needs a night out," he said as he shut the door.

Together, we all sighed with relief. "We did it!" Hannah cheered in a whisper.

The next morning bright and early Dad made us pancakes — a little too early, to be honest. When we came into the kitchen, he was already serving Ren. "I've decided to go back to college," he said, holding out his plate for Dad to fill. "Last night got me thinking. High school rocked but it's time to leave it to sis. I'm thinking I might have a career ahead in surveillance."

"I hear PatrolTec has an opening," Hannah cracked and

we all tried hard not to giggle, thinking of Sherman and his flat tires. Dad looked out the window and saw the fort. "I knew that old fort was going to come down sooner or later," he commented.

Dad and Ren went off to discuss Ren's future when Mom came in to take over at the stove. She served pancakes to Farrah, Hannah, and Yancy and they took their plates to the breakfast nook. "So *exactly* what did you girls do last night?" Mom asked as she served me.

"Exactly?" I asked, not liking the suspicious look in her eyes.

She took my purple scarf from her robe pocket and draped it around my neck. "Exactly," she repeated.

I glanced at my friends chatting happily in the breakfast nook. I didn't want to get them in trouble, but I didn't like the idea of lying to Mom, either. Besides, I knew she had already figured out something had gone on. "Okay," I began, "Here's the thing, Mom. We left the house. But, I assure you, it was for a very important adolescent cause."

"Adolescent?" she questioned. Cringing, I waited for her to explode.

But, instead, her voice was calm. "Not too long ago I had a little girl who took ballet and did magic tricks," she said. "We cooked together in her Easy Bake oven and loved ponies and ladybugs." She blinked and for a second I thought I saw a tear in her eye. "I guess I missed the bridge between ladybugs and boys," she added.

"I think I'm still on that bridge," I admitted.

Mom hugged me to her and it felt good to have her so close. "Take your time crossing it," she advised.

Then I took my pancakes and joined my friends. After we were finished, I raised my orange juice for a toast. "To the unstoppable freshman!" I said.

"Unstoppable!" my friends toasted all together.

A car horn honked. "That's my mom," Farrah said, picking up her backpack by the kitchen door.

Yancy followed her. "She's giving me a ride," she said. I supposed she'd be back to pick up her dad's car later. I wondered if she'd tell him that she'd driven it. "Thanks for the party," she said as she left with Farrah. "It was truly life altering," she added, "better than any soap opera."

Hannah and I waved to her. We might have invited her as a replacement, but she'd be first choice with me and my friends from now on. Hannah turned to me and there was a sad look on her face. "My mom will be here any minute, too. We have to finish packing for the move."

That's when the reality of it all finally hit me. Hannah was really leaving. I didn't know how I was going to get through it without her. Somehow I'd have to, though.

We went back upstairs where she packed her things. Together we went to the front of the house and waited for her mother to arrive. "This is it," I said to her as her mother's car appeared down the road. "You're moving. Everything changes now."

"Everything would have changed anyway," she replied. "Last night did that." She wrapped her arms around me a squeezed tight. "Don't worry," she whispered. "You're ready for high school."

As she pulled out of the hug, she slipped a sticker picture from her camera into my hand. It was a photo of the four of us squeezed into the little car. "Don't forget," she said.

"Never," I promised.

Then Hannah jumped into the car with her mom and, with a last wave, she was gone. I stood there, gazing down at the picture in my hand and thinking about everything that had happened.

When Yancy jumped into the display window at the mall, it surprised me. And last night, I had surprised myself. I only knew that I didn't want to lose that part of myself I'd discovered.

I went upstairs to my bedroom and plopped down on my bed. There was still one thing I felt badly about — I still hadn't been kissed. I'd come so close, too.

Something shone into my window, like a reflection from something metallic. I went to my window and looked out. There, in the fort window, was the crown from last night.

How had that gotten there?

Wondering, I climbed out the window and crossed the porch roof. I was reaching for the crown, when a hand reached out. It was Steve! He had been in the fort, but now he stepped out onto the roof with me and placed the crown on my head. "This belongs to you," he said — and he kissed me.

And so it happened — the girl in the lopsided crown got her kiss. And you'll just have to take my word for it. As first kisses go, it was completely perfect.